JOHNNY REED'S CAT
AND OTHER NORTHERN TALES

KATHLEEN HERSOM

Illustrated by P J Lynch

A & C BLACK · LONDON

To George English with many thanks for his infinite patience in recording these tales for Radio Newcastle.

First published 1987 by A & C Black (Publishers) Ltd,
35 Bedford Row, London WC1R 4JH

Text Copyright © 1987 Kathleen Hersom
Illustrations © 1987 P J Lynch

British Library Cataloguing in Publication Data
Hersom, Kathleen
  Johnny Reed's cat and other northern tales.
  I. Title II. Lynch, P.J., 1962–
823'.914 [J] PZ7

  ISBN 0-7136-2773-5

Filmset by August Filmsetting, Haydock, St. Helens
Printed in Great Britain by R J Acford Ltd., Chichester, Sussex

Contents

Introduction

All of these retellings of legends and folk-tales have been broadcast by Radio Newcastle under the title of 'Northern Tales', and I am indebted to Virtue Jones of the BBC and the late Herbert Sutherland of Newcastle Polytechnic for their encouragement and help in making the collection.

Folk-tales are universal and their roots spread wide. The claim of these tales to be 'northern' is made only because the versions on which they are based happen to have their roots in Northumberland and County Durham. The number of places in Britain claiming to be the final resting place of King Arthur is notorious. *The Elves and the Shoemaker*, collected by the Brothers Grimm, is an echo of Durham's *Cauld Lad of Hylton*, just as their *Mother Holle* may be a German *Ji-jaller Bag* . . . or, perhaps, the other way round.

So it would be hazardous to insist on any story belonging uniquely to any particular district. Even some stories about such an essentially north-eastern saint as Saint Cuthbert might possibly be matched elsewhere.

They were selected and rewritten from the earliest written sources available, with a young audience in mind, though the old tales from which they were derived were originally told orally for the entertainment of a whole community.   *K.H.*

How Eilaf became Eilaf Dodds

It happened far back in the time when the monks were fleeing from the Danes who were plundering our English monasteries for their treasure. People had only one name each in those days; just a Christian name when they were Christian, and just a name when they were not; but never a surname.

Now Eilaf was a monk from the island of Lindisfarne, one of several monks who had been wandering on the mainland for some years, between Scotland and Yorkshire, taking with them a coffin. In the coffin was the body of Saint Cuthbert with some relics of other saints; for when Cuthbert lay dying, two hundred years earlier, he had begged the brethren to take him with them if they ever had to flee before the Vikings. And their successors had not forgotten the promise that had been given.

But famine and pestilence were spreading throughout the north. Although the country people were good to them, giving them linen and wool, cheese, bread and milk they could ill afford themselves, many of the monks died. Those who survived were very weary, sick, and discouraged.

At last the little band of survivors, with their precious coffin, had dwindled to four.

One of the four was certainly Eilaf. The other three may well have been Edmund and Hunred and Stitheard, for those are all likely Anglo-Saxon names, as good as any other.

All four were quite exhausted by hunger. The season of berries and mushrooms was over, and for the winter that lay ahead, there was nothing left in the wicker basket that was slung beneath the cart, but a single cheese and a salted horse's head.

For nearly a week, Eilaf's stomach had been shouting pantry. And every time it shouted pantry he saw that cheese in his mind's eye, and he smelled that cheese in his mind's nose; and he longed for it more than he longed for his soul's salvation. And he forgot the commandment, 'Thou shalt not steal', as completely as he had forgotten the hour of his birth.

So one morning, when Edmund and Hunred and Stitheard had closed their eyes in prayer, Eilaf crept up to the cart, and quietly removed the cheese from the basket, hugging it fondly to himself beneath his habit.

When the prayers were ended, the four set off once more on their weary hunt for food, with Eilaf lagging well behind. He was pulling off little nibbles of cheese as he walked. Very, very tasty. He called out to the others that his feet were hurting him.

By noon they had found nothing. The only farm they had passed was in ruins. Edmund and Hunred and Stitheard sat down in hungry despair, in that desolate place. Eilaf was quite out of sight. The other three did not know that he had been looking for a secret hiding place for the cheese, among the boulders behind them.

'If we do not eat soon, we will be as dead as Saint Cuthbert and all the others in the coffin,' said Edmund. 'Let us have just a little of our cheese now, before we die of starvation.'

So the brethren knelt down and said a long grace, and then Edmund went to the wicker basket to fetch the cheese; but the salted horse's head was lying lonely in the basket by itself, for there *was* no cheese.

'We have been robbed!' said Edmund. 'Our cheese has been stolen!' Hunred and Stitheard were ready to cry with anger and

disappointment, for they were all as weak as babies with hunger and weariness.

Then the three thin, empty monks began to rage at the thief, and to say what should happen to such a wicked sinner; and they could not, with charity, think of a punishment severe enough for him.

'Saint Cuthbert should change him into—into—into—a mouse!' Edmund spluttered angrily.

'Or—a rat?' suggested Hunred.

'I wish Saint Cuthbert would change the thief into a *fox*!' said Stitheard. And the other two agreed that to be changed into a fox would be a fitting punishment for stealing the last cheese from four hungry men. So, there and then, they knelt down and prayed, but with little hope, for the thief to be changed into a fox.

But Edmund opened one eye before 'Amen' and from the corner of that eye he could see that there was something prowling stealthily through the heather.

It was a red fox, with the identical stolen cheese in its jaws!

Edmund opened his other eye very wide and nudged Hunred. 'Look! The fox!' he whispered.

Hunred opened both his eyes very wide and nudged Stitheard. 'Look! The fox!' he whispered.

'It is the thief!' said Stitheard, poking Hunred in his skinny ribs.

'It is the thief!' repeated Hunred, poking Edmund in *his* skinny ribs.

Then they laughed, till the tears jerked down their cheeks, happy that their prayers had been answered, and at the antics of the fox, who could neither devour nor get rid of the cheese, which was both sticky and crumbly, so that it clung in part to his sharp teeth, and in part it fell to the ground.

After a minute or two, Edmund looked all round and said 'But where is Brother Eilaf?'

And then it was that the monks realised that Eilaf was not with them, and had not been there when they said grace, or when they found that the cheese was missing; and they remembered the lagging behind, and the sore feet excuse, and they all cried out together, 'Brother Eilaf is the thief!' And the thought that it was Eilaf writhing and squirming in front of them, made them merrier still.

Then, when the red fox had slunk away, and the brethren had laughed away all their weariness and ill-humour, they prayed to God and Saint Cuthbert to restore Eilaf to his human shape; for they were all good-natured men, not given to bearing grudges.

And, once more, they believed that their prayer was answered, for the next time they saw Eilaf he was looking like himself, instead of like a fox; though still, perhaps, a little reddish in the face, as well he might.

Later, in the twelfth century, there was an old monk, called Reginald of Durham, who wrote about all these happenings. He tells us that, 'from that day, all the race of Eilaf bore the name of Tod (or Dodd) which, in the mother tongue, signifies a fox.' So today you will come across people called Todd, or Dodd, or Dodds (which are different names all with the same meaning) in any part of the country, but most of all in Northumberland, all descended from Eilaf.

THE LITTLE DUN COW

About a thousand years ago, there was a bonny dun-coloured cow who lived near a hill. A hill called Wardelaw. Some people say that was the place we call Warden Law today, and others say it was probably the old hill that is known as Maiden Castle, close by Durham City. Choose which you will, it was a wild sort of place.

But Durham City itself was not there in those days; no Cathedral, no Castle, no big green man on a big green horse prancing in the Market Place. There was only a great wooded hill that the Saxons called Dunholm; a wild, craggy, scratchy place with the river Wear running almost all the way round it. Fierce animals prowled beneath. Wolves and wild boars sheltered among the crags bordering the river banks, and jackdaws nested in the cliffs. They were the great-great-greatest grandfathers of the jackdaws who are building their nests this year, just a few hundred feet higher up, in the Cathedral tower. They can be seen on many a breezy day, playing their tumbling floating games between the pinnacles and the sky.

Our dun cow was only a little cow, because at that time all the cows and sheep and horses were a good deal smaller than those that you see in the fields nowadays. Even the people were not so tall then as they are today.

She was a friendly, good-tempered beast, and a splendid milker. But, like you and me, this little cow wasn't absolutely perfect. Her most troublesome failing was that she was so fidgety and restless. Never content to stay near home, she was always wandering away, driving the busy cow-woman to her wits' end.

As there were neither fields nor hedges, the cow-woman's children took turns to mind the cows during the day, and keep a look-out for hungry wolves.

'Don't you dare lose sight of them cows,' she warned them,

'or I'll wallop you! And, whatever else you do, don't you ever take your eyes off that plaguy dun cow!'

Most of the time the children were very good at minding the cows, but no sooner did a boy's attention wander, than the dun cow would be off and out of sight beyond the bushes. She was never able to get far away because she would soon be missed, and then the cow-woman and the cow-woman's children would come running, and waving, and bawling, and home she had to go.

At last the angry cow-woman grew tired of walloping the children and walloping the cow each time she strayed, so, in desperation she fetched a piece of rope and tethered her to a tree.

But early one fine spring morning, before the flies became bothersome, the cow managed to break loose from her tree, and for a long time no one noticed that she was missing. I have no idea what could have kept them all looking so busily in the opposite direction, but, for once, she was able to get clear away.

She had never felt so happy and free. It was peaceful being out of earshot of the scolding cow-wife and her quarrelsome children, and hearing nothing but the larks rising, or occasionally the sudden sucking sound of her own hooves in squelchy places.

She enjoyed plodging splashily through the bogs and the little burns where she would stop to drink. Sometimes too, she would pause to rub herself against a tree trunk or a low branch, for she was a very itchy little cow, and the flies became more troublesome as the sun got higher.

But mostly she ate, and kept moving. The next bite of grass always looked greener and juicier than the last bite, and so she munched her way steadily across the miles that lay between Wardelaw and Dunholm.

Once she saw a woman approaching her. The woman slowed down when she saw the dun cow, and then came closer to have a better look. The back legs of the cow were friendly and inquisitive and wanted to go forward to meet the woman, but the front legs wondered whether she was a shouter and a walloper like the cow-woman, and would rather have run away. So all four legs stood stock still, except for twitches, while the dun cow stared back.

Now if you have ever tried to stare out a cow, you will remember that just as you think you have won, and that the cow is going to turn away, she will defy you by licking her nose at you—first a lick up to the right—then a lick up to the left—then right again. That is a very clever and annoying trick on the cow's part, because it is something you cannot possibly do back, no matter how hard you try. The cow-woman's children could no more do it than you can.

At last the woman sniffed, and went on her way, just as the cow gave a fly-flick with her tail and went on hers. So it was a draw.

The little cow soon reached the shaggy undergrowth that surrounded Dunholm. It seemed dark as a cave after the bright sunshine. For a long time she buffeted about among the bushes and young trees, getting nowhere. Her usual good temper was becoming strained. She would have liked to get out and back into open country, but she couldn't find the way. Her horns kept catching on things.

At last she saw sunshine again in a level open space. She had reached the high plateau where there was bracken, and grass, and cowslips with bees inside them, and more than enough room for one little cow to sit down and chew the cud, which is what she did. It was a long time since she had had a sit down.

She blinked as she ruminated, enjoying the warmth of the sun, and listening to the waves slapping on the river far below. Two or three deer came to look at her, but she soon stared them back under cover.

Now it was not only the dun cow who was seeking a peaceful resting place that fine morning. A Bishop called Aldhun and five hundred monks from the abbey at Ripon were making their way to Chester-le-Street. For years they had been moving from here to there, and from there to here, in fear of the Norsemen who were plundering the monasteries and doing much harm. Wherever the monks went they took with them the bones of good Saint Cuthbert of Lindisfarne, in a wooden coffin. For, before he died, Saint Cuthbert had told them that if they had to flee from the enemy, his body should go with them. But now peace had been made with the Danes, they were free to return home at last.

So on this bright morning Bishop Aldhun and his five hundred monks arrived at the hill called Wardelaw. You will remember that that was the home of the restless little cow. And there the cart that carried Saint Cuthbert's coffin stuck fast and could not be moved. You would think that five hundred men, and their beasts as well, could have pushed and pulled it on its way. But although relays of the youngest and strongest heaved and thrust till the sweat ran down them like rivers, they could not budge that cart. It seemed as though Saint Cuthbert did not want to go back to Chester-le-Street.

They fasted for three days and nights. And they prayed for help. Then one of the monks had a dream, or vision. And in this vision he learned that they must take Saint Cuthbert's body to a place called Dunholm, where it would remain forever.

'Praise the Lord!' said Bishop Aldhun. 'Let us go to Dunholm without delay, and build a shrine for holy Cuthbert there.'

But the Bishop did not know that part of the country himself, so he asked the monks which of them could lead the way to Dunholm. But all the monks shrugged their shoulders, shook their heads in turn, and said, 'I have never heard of Dunholm, I am a stranger here too.' So there they were, glum and hungry and weary. They knew at last where they must go, but had no understanding of how to get there.

Suddenly they were startled by the harsh voice of the cow-woman.

'Hi there!' she shouted to a neighbour. 'Hast seen me dun cow anywhere?'

'Why aye!' her neighbour called back. 'I saw her a while since, up at Dunholm.'

Now you have probably guessed, quite rightly, that this was the woman who had looked so hard at the little dun cow as she approached Dunholm.

When the monks heard the name 'Dunholm', they forgot their blistered feet, and their hunger, and their weary bones. They gathered up their habits and ran to where the two women were standing.

'Pray good women,' they begged. 'Will you tell us the way to the place you call Dunholm? We have great need to go there, but we are all strangers here, and we do not know which way to turn.'

'You had best go with the cow-wife,' said the second woman. 'She is going to Dunholm now, to seek her cow.'

Then the brothers found that the cart with the coffin moved easily again, as if it had been newly greased. So the five hundred monks, and their Bishop, and the remains of Saint Cuthbert followed the cow-woman all the way to Dunholm. There they found the wayward little cow trying to lick an itch that was just out of reach. You know how it is with cows. No doubt she was alarmed to find herself surrounded by such a great excited congregation, all chattering away like a flock of starlings at dusk.

What happened to the dun cow after that, it is hard to discover. Although many people still repeat the legend, and there are thick and thin books in the reference library about her, the story always ends here. Let us hope she was treated very kindly for the rest of her life. The monks would, no doubt, see to that, for by straying she had done them a great service.

But where the cow's story ends, Durham's story begins. For

the monks set down Saint Cuthbert's coffin right on the high cliffs above the river Wear where they found the dun cow chewing her cud, and licking her itch. They built a little shrine over it, of wands and branches, which lasted until they were able to make a bigger, stronger church of wood. That lasted until a stone church was built, and that lasted until the building of the great Cathedral itself. And for close on nine hundred years the Cathedral has stood above the tomb of Saint Cuthbert. Alongside it was built the Castle, and around it grew the city, houses, and shops, and churches, and schools, and a University.

If you ever come to Durham, you must visit the Cathedral. And when you have paid your respects to Saint Cuthbert, and the Venerable Bede, you must come out of the great north door with its Sanctuary knocker, and turn down to the right-hand corner of Palace Green. You will find yourself in Dun Cow Lane. Look up to your right, and you will see the dun cow's story, carved in stone, against the wall of the Cathedral.

Learned people will tell you that this is a phoney no-good sort of statue, because the cow-woman and her companion are wearing clothes that are far too modern—too modern by about eight hundred years. And, in spite of having lost her right ear, the dun cow herself looks far too fine a specimen of the seventeenth century Durham shorthorn breed to be a scrawny little Saxon cow.

I expect they are right. They have passed their examinations and should know. But even if it isn't all historically accurate, you must admit that the mason has done a very fine job in making the cow-woman look disagreeable enough to drive any self-respecting cow all of the eight miles from Warden Law to Durham—and in making the dun cow look as happy and proud as she deserves to be ... even though the swishing of her tail suggests that those wretched flies still seem to be bothering her.

The Brown Man of the Moors, the Cowt of Kielder, and Lord Soulis

Long ago there was a mighty Northumbrian chieftain called the Cowt of Kielder. 'Cowt' means a colt, and he was called the Cowt because he was as strong and lively as a young horse—and he was a great deal bigger than an ordinary man, too. His castle of Kielder was the last English stronghold before the troublesome Scottish border. On the other side, in Liddesdale, a mighty Scottish chieftain called Lord Soulis lived in a bleak square castle called Hermitage, which was the last Scottish stronghold before the troublesome English border. There was no love lost between the two of them.

Now one fine morning the Cowt rose early to go hunting. When his gentle wife learned that he intended crossing the border into Liddesdale, she begged him to be content with following the English stags up Tynedale or by Kielder Water; for she feared that Lord Soulis would surely challenge his trespassing, and then the Cowt might never return to her. She knew that the Scottish chieftain wielded an axe of magic strength, and had a charmed sword with a hilt of adderstone.

But the Cowt only laughed at her fears and said, 'So now! *I* shall wear my suit of enchanted mail, and my helmet of sand that was spun by a mermaid on the ocean bed. I shall wear holly and rowan in my helmet, so what strength or magic can harm me then?'

And away he galloped with his huntsmen and his hounds, heading for Liddesdale.

When they came to the place on the high moor that is called Redswire, the Cowt blew a joyful blast on his bugle horn, and as he blew, a curlew dropped from the sky, circling round him with its harsh wild cry.

He blew a second blast, and at once the fresh breeze dropped, so that not a breath of air could be felt—and yet, contrariwise, the fronds of the bracken waved wildly to and fro, as though tossed by a violent gale.

A third time the Cowt blew on his bugle, and the bracken became still once more, and there beside him stood a swarthy creature, half the size of a man, and the hair of his head was frizzly red, and a red hedgehog hung cowering on his arm.

At the sight of him the hounds howled miserably, and hung back as though they sensed some evil in their way.

The surly creature scowled at the Cowt and demanded,

Why rises high the stag-hounds' cry
Where stag-hounds ne'er should be?
Why wakes the horn the silent morn
Without the leave of me?

Then the Cowt suspected that his dwarf must be one of that tribe of evil spirits that was thrust out of heaven, long ago, by the Archangel Michael. He knew that a few of them had landed on lonely moorlands, and had stayed on in the shape of dwarfs, and brownies, causing nothing but trouble, holding jealously to their territory, and resenting any mortals who hunted over it.

When the Cowt asked the dwarf his name, he replied that he was called the Brown Man of the Moors, and woe betide any hunter who poached on his moorland!

The Cowt, who was not at all afraid of the angry little spirit, was about to say so, plainly and boldly, when the Brown Man and his hedgehog disappeared, leaving no trace of where they had gone.

The huntsmen and their hounds bounded on until they came to the Kielder Stone, a massive stone that stood lonely among the heather then, as it does today. They rode three times round the stone from east to west, as the sun goes, for they knew that to ride widdershins, or the opposite way, would bring

disaster; and as they rode round it the Cowt heard a low voice murmuring, 'I come for death, I come to work thy woe!' and he knew then that the Spirit of the Stone, who lived underneath there, was the Brown Man of the Moors.

Even so, the bold Cowt did not turn back, but led his hunting party on into Liddesdale. As they approached Hermitage Castle they saw a Scottish knight riding towards them. When the messenger was within speaking distance of the huntsmen he called to them, saying, 'I greet your master well, from Lord Soulis of Liddesdale. He heard your bugle horn, and bids you welcome to his festive hall.' This was an unexpectedly friendly message from his old enemy, and, wisely, the Cowt was very wary of it. However, he told the huntsmen to accept the invitation graciously, but to be on their guard and beware of magic.

When they entered Hermitage, a fine feast was set before the Cowt and his men. The blood-red wine flowed freely, and the minstrels played and sang, so that the hall was filled with laughter and music.

Suddenly, the tapers went out, and the minstrels fell silent. The blood in the huntsmen's veins ran ice-cold, so that their hands clutching their short swords became quite rigid. They tried to rise from their seats, but found themselves sealed to the benches like statues.

Only the Cowt, saved by his charmed armour, was free to rise. He burst through the door, out into the open, his bloodhound bounding before him. Lord Soulis followed with his men-at-arms.

Outside the castle a terrible skirmish took place between the Cowt and the Scottish soldiers, the Cowt carving a bloody passage through the men in his bid for freedom. But in the turmoil the little Brown Man of the Moors sidled up to Lord Soulis and whispered in his ear that a charmed suit of mail was protecting the Cowt from the Scottish weapons, and reminded the lord that no magic could withstand running water.

Acting on the Brown Man's advice, Lord Soulis and his men, so many against one, drove the Cowt towards the river that is called Hermitage Water. There the Cowt stumbled and fell, sprawling into the stream. The holly and rowan floated away. And the Scottish lances pierced the Cowt's armour, for the magic of it was powerless against the running water.

Soon the brave Cowt lay dead in the stream, and the place where he died was known ever after as Cowt's Linn. He was buried on the bank nearby, and the huge mound of grave, with a stone at the head and another at the foot, is still to be seen.

The English huntsmen, still holding their bugle horns and with their keen hounds at their feet, will remain in their deathly sleep till the ruined tower of Hermitage falls down.

As for Lord Soulis, so many complaints about him and his villainous ways were brought to the Scottish King, Robert the Bruce, that finally, in a burst of irritation he exclaimed, 'Oh boil him if it pleases you, but let me hear no more of him!'

So they took him at his word, and boiled the tyrant to death in a huge cauldron, up on the moors at Nine Stane Rig.

The king was horrified when he heard how literally his words had been taken, and he sent messengers at once to countermand the order. But they came too late. Lord Soulis was dead.

So the two chieftains each came to a bad end, and though two bad ends never make one good end, they do make a very definite end to the story of the Brown Man of the Moors, the Cowt of Kielder, and Lord Soulis.

CUNNING DICK

Centuries ago there was a robber who lived by himself in Staward Pele—the old pele tower that was built on a wooded crag high above the river Allen, where it still stands today, a lonely ruin.

Behind his back he was known as Cunning Dick, but to his face everyone called him Dicky—Dicky of Kingswood.

Now, robber or no robber, there was something to be said for Dicky, because he was not a violent thief, as thieves go. He always boasted that he was just not interested in bloodshed. He was interested, however, in other people's belongings. Very interested he was, roaming far through Northumberland, and beyond, to see what he could see, and find what he could find. He took what he needed and kept what he got. He was, it must be admitted, a bit of a rogue, and a good deal of a rapscallion.

One day, he happened to be in Denton Burn, not far from the city of Newcastle; and happening to look through a hedge, he just happened to see a bonny pair of fat red oxen grazing in the field—all quite accidental, but up shot Cunning Dick's eyebrows, and, said he to himself,

'I could do with a pair of oxen just like them.'

Young Dicky wasn't the sort of simpleton who would help himself to another man's cattle in broad daylight, with inquisitive neighbours likely looking on, and the red-faced farmer himself, maybe, turning up at any moment to mend a fence, or fill a water-trough.

So he just picked himself a sprig of rowan to stick in his hat, to ward off the witches as all his fore-elders had done before him, and on he went down the Newcastle road, whistling as clear as a blackbird, to while away a few happy hours at the nearest inn. And when the few happy hours were whiled away, he stepped out into the night, and a blackness that suited his purpose precisely.

Back he went along the road, not whistling this time, but silent as a cloud, and stealthy as a fox, till he came to the field where the bonny red oxen were sitting down, either asleep, or not asleep—it was difficult to tell in a night as black as that night was.

Cunning Dick opened the gate wide, just as though the field belonged to him, and walking quietly up to the oxen, he spoke to them gently and respectfully, in the way he always spoke to animals. Saint Cuthbert himself, who tamed the wild birds and the seals by his gentleness, had not a kinder manner with them.

Then, without a sound, the oxen heaved themselves up, hind legs first, forelegs after, and plodded peaceably out of the field and on to the road where they waited patiently for Dicky to latch the gate behind them. And off they all ambled in a companionable silence in the direction of Carlisle, more like three friends taking a stroll together than a thief driving away his loot.

Dicky had taken good care not to be followed. He had planned with one of his drinking companions, that as soon as the farmer from Denton Burn discovered his loss, this young fellow would hint that he had seen his oxen, or some very like, far north, towards the Tweed.

So the poor farmer had gone off on a wild goose chase, fretting and fuming up to the north, while Cunning Dick and the oxen were driving steadily westwards.

After a deal of travelling, Dick decided that the money the oxen might fetch would be even more to his liking than the beasts themselves. So he made up his mind to sell them at the first opportunity.

Presently, as he was approaching Lanercost, he met an elderly farmer who stopped to admire the fine pair of oxen. Dicky coughed modestly, and agreed that they were very fine animals, but explained that, unfortunately, he was having to sell them to pay for the funeral of his dear old father, and to pay off all the debts that the old man had left behind him. If that was not a lie, it was an enormous stretch of the imagination, for the old man was dead and buried before ever Dicky was born, and he had never owed a farthing to anyone.

The old farmer was sympathetic, and offered Dick a fair price and a bit more for the cattle, and invited him back to his farm to seal the bargain in a mug of ale.

Dick had been much taken with the splendid mare that the farmer was riding. A fast-moving mare like that would be a great asset to a fellow like himself who sometimes needed to move away quickly out of a tight corner. So no sooner was he settled comfortably at the farmer's table, with the price of the oxen jingling in his purse, than he asked him if he had ever thought of selling his horse.

'Sell my mare!' said the old gentleman. 'I wouldn't sell that mare—not for a diamond as big as a brick! She's the finest mare in the county, and the best friend I ever had!'

'That's understandable,' said Dick craftily. 'I shouldn't want to sell her myself, if she were mine. But I hope you keep your stable bolted, for the country is full of thieves and scoundrels nowadays, and a mare like that must be a great temptation to an honest man. You know the saying, "It's no use bolting the stable-door after the horse has gone!"'

'But I don't keep her in a *stable*,' laughed the farmer. 'A stable is no place to house my best friend! I have built a manger for her in my bedroom, and there she stays with me the whole night through. I fall asleep to the soothing sound of her champing her oats, and the first thing I see when I wake is her two sharp ears twitching beyond the bedfoot.'

'Even so,' said Dicky, 'you could still lose your mare. Thieves and burglars do not stop short at bedrooms. I hope you sleep with your door bolted.'

'Bolted?' the farmer laughed, louder then ever. I would never trust my good friend to a simple bolt on the door! I have a lock, a patent, secret lock that no intruder could ever open. See here! This is how it works!'

And the silly, simple farmer took the padlock out of his pocket, and explained to Dicky every trick and detail of how it worked. And that was the end of the usefulness of that padlock, for a secret shared with a stranger isn't a secret any more.

So it was not surprising that next morning the poor, trusting old farmer woke, shivering with cold, to find his blankets scattered all over the floor and down the stairs, the house-door wide open, and the splendid mare—gone!

For Cunning Dick had climbed in through the window, spread the blankets to muffle the sound of hooves, led his prize down the stairs, and galloped away. He was now well on the road to Hexham.

Later that day, just as he was entering the town, whom should Dicky meet but the red-faced farmer from Denton Burn, who was still searching for his oxen. He had no idea who Dicky was, though Dicky knew fine well who he was.

'Good-day sir!' he called to the weary, travel-stained fellow. 'You are looking in a sorry way! Have you travelled far?'

'Indeed I have!' said the farmer, slumping down by the roadside. 'Half way round Northumberland and all to no purpose! Some rascally blackguard has stolen my two red oxen! Have you seen them by any chance? The finest beasts ever bred! Sleek and smooth as satin they were, except where the hair curled into tight rings on their brows; snow-white faces with gentle eyes; and a white plume at the end of their tails, combed smooth and soft like a girl's tresses; their backs and flanks are red, glowing red as a new-split horse chestnut; and four sturdy legs apiece, the firmest, sturdiest legs you ever did see, to bear the weight of those fine deep-chested animals; thick short horns, pointing safely downwards. Absolutely perfect, except for a small chip out of the left hind hoof of each. You never did see such animals in your life, I assure you, young man, and when I catch that rogue . . . !'

'Steady man, steady!' interrupted Dicky. 'You are mistaken! for I *did* see such animals! Two fine oxen, just as you describe; chestnut red, except for their white faces with the gentle eyes, and the white plume at the end of their tails; and the tight curls on their brows, and the deep chests, and the four sturdy legs apiece (for I counted them) and the little short horns pointing safely downwards; and a small chip, that I particularly noticed, out of the left hind hoof of each. I saw them, only this morning, grazing in a field next to the Priory at Lanercost. But if you would recover them you must hurry! That thief will be away across the border before nightfall, so you should be speeding on your way after him!'

Up jumped the hopeful farmer, all the weariness bounced out of him at the prospect of finding his oxen. But it was still a long way from Hexham to Lanercost, and the farmer looked enviously at Dicky's mount. A mare like that one would make short work of the miles separating him from his beloved oxen.

'Would you consider selling me your mare?' he asked. 'A steed like that would be worth a great deal to me at this moment, and I would pay you anything within reason to have her!'

Cunning Dick hawed and hummed, and pretended to be unwilling to part with such a fine animal, but finally named a sum which was certainly not within reason, not by any reckoning!

But the impatient farmer would have given away every guinea he possessed, if only he could reach Lanercost in time. So he willingly handed over the money, and galloped off westwards, leaving Dicky to chink his golden coins, and chuckle to himself in the roadway.

Riding at full cloppety-tilt, the farmer reached the place where his oxen were grazing, just before sunset. He lost no time in seeking out the owner of the field.

And when those two farmers came face to face, the one from Denton Burn, with the one from Lanercost, you can imagine the hullabaloo! For each believed himself to have been robbed by the other. What a shouting, and a threatening, and a swearing, and a shaking of fists, and a stamping of feet there was! Until at last each had bawled himself hoarse and breathless, and was ready to listen just a little more, and to shout just a little less.

Then, of course, they each found that the other was innocent, and that the villain who had swindled both of them was Cunning Dick—for each had paid him handsomely for what was not his to sell. So the two farmers apologised, and swapped the animals over, and shook hands, and slapped one another on the back, and vowed what they would do to Dicky if they ever found him.

But they never did. He probably slipped quietly away into those wild border hills that were called the Debatable Lands, where his cattle-reiving ancestors used to live, for he was never seen again at Staward Pele or Kingswood. Maybe he reformed his ways and settled down to earn an honest living, and, maybe he didn't. Nobody knows.

Johnny Reed's Cat

Johnny Reed was, at one time, the sexton at the village of Stain-drop, in County Durham. He had a cat of which he was particularly fond. She was a comfortable, homely black cat with one white paw, but there was nothing in any way remarkable about her—just a good plain cat to keep the mice down, and purr by the fireside, making the place feel like home.

One evening, at the cold time of the year, Johnny Reed was working late at the grave-digging, and had to finish off by lantern light, so that all would be ready for a burying in the morning.

When all was done, he cleaned his tools, put them away, and set off towards home, thinking of nothing but the hot supper that would be waiting for him in the warm kitchen.

As he went down the road he came to a field-gate; a gate he knew well enough for he passed it at least twice a day. But this evening there was an unusual dark shadow beside it. In the shadow there seemed to be strange bright lights—some darting about, some burning still and steadily.

'What's here?' said Johnny Reed to himself. 'Fire-flies? glow-worms?' And he went closer to have a better look.

The shadow looked darker, and the lights looked brighter, and when he got really close he saw that it wasn't a shadow at all, but a crowd of black tom-cats—nine of them—all with golden-green eyes; some cats sitting still, some cats dicky-dancing about.

'Swiiiiii———sh!' said Johnny Reed, thinking to scatter the cats.

But the cats took no notice at all. Some stayed sitting still, some carried on dicky-dancing about.

Then he heard someone calling him,

'Johnny Reed! Johnny Reed!'

'Hallo there,' said Johnny Reed, talking to himself,

'Someone wants us?' and he looked back the way he'd come, but there was no one following him from the churchyard.

Then he heard it again,

'Johnny Reed! Johnny Reed!'

'All right,' said Johnny, talking to himself, 'I'm coming, I'm coming!' and he looked up the road, the way his cottage lay, but there was no one calling him along there.

Once more he heard it.

'Johnny Reed! Johnny Reed!'

'*Now* where are you?' said Johnny, talking to himself, and he looked over the hedge to see if there was a boy behind it, playing a trick on him. But there wasn't one.

'Well!' said Johnny, staring at the nine black tom-cats. 'Was it one of you wanting me?' And it was still himself he was talking to, because Johnny Reed wasn't the sort of man who'd really expect an answer from a party of cats.

So he nearly jumped out of his skin when the biggest, blackest tom-cat said,

'Yes, it was!'

Now Johnny Reed had never in his life, been spoken to by a cat; but he reckoned that any cat who had learned to speak good plain English ought to be treated with respect.

So he took off his cap, which was half way to being off already, for his hair was standing that much on end—and he asked the cat, very humbly, what he could do for him.

'Not much,' said the cat, 'But
Johnny Reed! Johnny Reed!
Tell Madame Momfoot
That Mally Dixon's deed!'

Now Johnny Reed had never heard of Madame Momfoot, nor Mally Dixon either, but he thought he'd better sound willing to do what the cat wanted, so he said, 'Yes, I will.'

Then off he ran, glad to get away from talking cats, home to his little old wife, and his own ordinary quiet cat, and his warm fireside.

As soon as he had got enough breath back to speak, he asked his wife if she had ever heard, in her gossiping round the neighbourhood, of a Madame Momfoot, or a Mally Dixon.

His wife laughed and said, 'Madame Momfoot indeed! There's a fancy name for you! I'm sure I never heard tell of such a one in *these* parts! Nor of Mally Dixon neither! Who was it asking for them?'

But when Johnny Reed said, 'It was a big black tom-cat,' she looked at him as though she was thinking that maybe he wasn't,

after all, the sensible man she had always taken him to be.

So then Johnny Reed told her the story from beginning to end, and when he came to the part where the cat said,

'Tell Madame Momfoot

That Mally Dixon's deed!'

up jumped his own quiet cat from the fireside and said, '*Is* she then? Then *I* must be off!' And away she bolted out of the house, never to be seen again.

Now it has never been decided whether Johnny Reed's cat was really just a cat, or some sort of a fairy disguised as a cat. But, either way, it seems certain that her name was Madame Momfoot, and that she left in a hurry to attend the funeral of her sister, or a very dear friend called Mally Dixon. For, although Johnny Reed and his wife enquired all round the district, nobody anywhere near Staindrop knew anything of a Madame Momfoot or a Mally Dixon.

As for the strange mourners by the field-gate, they were never seen again either!

THE BISHOP AND THE BRAWN

There was once a fierce wild boar who was covered with bristles. His tusks were as long as the horns of Highland cattle. His eyes were evil and watchful and smaller than a hedgehog's. He was bigger than the biggest pig there ever was in the County Show. He was a fast runner. And he smelt horrible.

This boar, or brawn, roamed the countryside just beyond the Bishop of Durham's castle, at Bishop Auckland. He went around uprooting the crops, damaging the woodland, and killing any of the Bishop's tenants who did not get out of his way fast enough.

In those days, the Bishops of Durham were called Prince Bishops, for not only were they rich as princes, but most of the land in the county belonged to them, and they owned a few castles and many houses as well. They had their own armies, and they minted their own money. They were as powerful inside their own bishopric as the King of England was outside it.

The Bishop of Durham determined to be rid of this great brawn, and promised a handsome reward to anyone who could kill the monstrous beast.

Now there was, at this time, a young knight called Pollard who was both clever and brave. He made up his mind to kill the brawn, and earn the prize.

So this is what he did.

First, he took time and trouble to study the habits of the brawn, stalking him from a safe distance, to find where his favourite tracks and feeding grounds were.

Pollard discovered that during the day the brawn slept heavily in his lair, beneath the beech trees in the forest at Etherley Dene. But at night he went hunting for food, and although he ate a variety of things, it was beech mast that he ate with the greatest joy and excitement.

So this is what Pollard did next.

He rode away to a beech forest that was beyond the brawn's hunting ground, and there he collected a great sackful of ripe beech mast.

Then one clear night he armed himself with a broad curved blade called a falchion, filled his wallet with cheese and oatcake for himself, and carried the sack to the lair at Etherley Dene, while the old brawn was rootling away at the far end of the forest. And there he emptied his sack at the foot of a tall beech tree.

Taking the empty sack with him to soften his sitting a little, he climbed up the tree, perched on a stout branch, and ate just enough of his cheese and oatcake to keep himself going till the next time, and settled down to wait for his enemy.

It was almost dawn before the brawn came back to his lair at a waddling trot.

Pollard was stiff and cold with waiting.

First he heard him, crackling through the undergrowth.

Then he smelt him.

Then he saw him.

The brawn was blown and heavy from his night's guzzling, and his little eyes appeared even smaller than usual; but when they lighted on the great heap of beech mast, he ran forward with eager grunts and squeals to bury his snout in it.

Pollard watched fascinated, as the greedy animal slurped and snorted, sucking in and puffing out, as though his stomach was empty as empty, instead of being as full as full. Twitches of greedy excitement ruffled along his skin from time to time, and his ears flapped in tune with his jaws.

At last, when the heap of beech mast had dwindled almost to nothing, and the brawn was searching about for the last few nuts, Pollard shook all the branches within his reach, so that a shower of ripe mast dropped down from the tree. It seemed impossible that the brawn would have room for any more, yet this windfall too, was devoured eagerly. Then, stupefied with his gluttony, he sank down into his lair, and fell asleep.

Pollard climbed down quietly from his tree, and armed only with his falchion, attacked the great lump.

The brawn, although bewildered by such a sudden awakening, and heavy with gorging, charged tuskily, almost throwing Pollard off balance.

But he quickly recovered, and returned to the attack. If the brawn had not been so full of food he would have made short work of Pollard; as it was they were evenly matched.

For hours they fought there, hammer and tongs, in Etherley Dene. Sometimes the brawn gained ground, sometimes Pollard did. They both weakened as day wore on, but neither gave up the struggle even when night fell. But it was Pollard who gave the final blow that felled the brawn dead at his feet.

By that time the young man was too exhausted to return to Auckland Castle to claim his prize. All he wanted to do was to lie down and sleep and sleep and sleep.

So after taking a few bites of his cheese and oatcake, he cut out the brawn's tongue, slipped it into his wallet, lay down in the shelter of some tall bracken, and fell at once into a very deep sleep.

Some few hours later a travelling stranger rode through the forest. He had passed through Bishop Auckland earlier that morning, and heard about the ferocious brawn, and the price that had been set on his head.

'Here's luck for me!' he said to himself when he saw the huge carcass of the brawn lying across his path.

'This must be the very brawn that has been causing so much havoc hereabouts. He must have met with some other wild animal in the forest, and fought to the death. All I have to do is to cut off the head and claim my reward from the Bishop of Durham!'

So without more ado, he drew his sword, slashed off the head, and galloped off with it to Auckland Castle, without noticing the real killer of the brawn asleep among the bracken.

It was several hours later that Pollard woke refreshed from his long sleep.

When he saw that the brawn had been beheaded, and that there were freshly printed hoofmarks on the ground, he guessed what might have happened.

'Ah well!' he thought. 'Whoever's taken the head, has not got the whole of it, but there is no time to be lost in claiming my reward.'

So off he ran at high speed, to the Bishop's castle.

He arrived panting, just in the nick of time, for there in the great hall was the travelling stranger, presenting the Bishop with the brawn's head, and making a fine modest speech about how he had slain the brute single-handed.

And there, too, was the Bishop accepting it most gratefully, and complimenting the stranger on his courage, and saying he should have a reward worthy of such a gallant deed.

'I beg your pardon, my Lord Bishop,' said Pollard, who had pushed past the servants, and only just recovered enough puff to speak, 'but there seems to have been a mistake. It is I, and not this stranger, who has slain the brawn!'

'You!' said the Bishop. 'A fine tale indeed! See! Here is the severed head of the brawn, brought to me by this gentleman. There is no mistaking those villainous tusks, or this enormous head—how can you doubt the truth of his tale?'

'I doubt it by this!' said Pollard pulling the brawn's tongue out of his wallet.

'Here is the tongue of the brawn that I battled with for a

whole day and half a night before I slew him. I cut out this tongue before resting from the struggle. If you will but examine the brawn's head that the stranger has brought you, you will find that it has no tongue!'

The Bishop opened the jaws of the brawn, and there, sure enough, between the rows of sharp teeth, in the place where the tongue should have been, was nothing at all.

The travelling stranger, in spite of the fine modest speech he had just made, seemed to have lost *his* tongue as well. For he left the castle at great speed, without so much as excusing himself to the Bishop, or even wishing him good-bye. He rode break-neck-or-nowt back to Mitford, where he belonged, and was never again seen in those parts.

'You have, indeed, deserved a good reward,' the Bishop said to Pollard. 'And this is what it is: I am going now, to my dinner, and as much land as you can ride around, while I am still dining, will be yours to keep, for ever. So choose your ride carefully.'

Now, in those times, dinners, for those who could afford them, lasted a long, long time. Not only were there many courses, but helpings were large.

The Bishop was willing to make his meal last even longer than usual, for he was sincerely grateful to Pollard for ridding the land of the beastly brawn.

So he took his time, thinking that Pollard, as well as his own digestion, would benefit by the extra chewing.

However, he was soon surprised to learn from his serving-man, that the young hunter had finished his ride, and was already returned. He was waiting in an anteroom, until the Bishop had finished his meal.

Curious to know why he had come back so early, the Bishop pushed his plate aside, wiped his mouth, and summoned Pollard into the hall.

'You have been away a very short time,' he said. 'You can only have had time to ride round a very small piece of land. Tell me, where did you go?'

'I just rode once around Auckland Castle, Your Lordship,' answered Pollard. 'It did not take me long.'

The Bishop, at first, was flabbergasted. Then he began to chuckle and splutter with amusement. He ordered another glass, and more wine to be brought in.

Then, offering a glass of wine to Pollard, he said,

'You were too clever for the brawn, and now you have been too clever for me! To keep my bargain, I would have to give up my Bishop's palace to you. But I have an alternative to suggest, an alternative you may prefer. Come outside, and I will give you another choice.'

So the Bishop led the way out of the castle, till he came to a place where there was a wide view of meadows and woodland and pasture.

'Here are five hundred acres of fine farmland,' he said. 'Would that be a fair exchange? I think it could be more use to you than a castle.'

Pollard, indeed, thought so too.

So the Bishop gave him that fine fertile farmland for his family to keep for generation after generation.

Pollard built a splendid house on it, and cultivated the land with care. His descendants lived there for many centuries, and though his family has now died out, the land that was once theirs can still be shown, and is known, even today as Pollard's Lands.

Lord Bateman and Susie Pye

Lord Bateman of Northumberland was a wealthy, lively young man who loved travel and adventure. So, one day he set sail for Turkey in search of it.

But the adventure he found there was not a happy one, for he was seized by a rich and savage Turk, and thrown into a dungeon.

There he was chained to a log, and there he lived on bread and water for seven weary years.

Now this savage Turk had an only daughter, a kind and beautiful girl called Susie Pye. If you think that Susie Pye is an unlikely name for a Turkish maiden, never mind! That is the name she had.

One day, when Susie Pye was passing near the dungeon, a sad murmuring came to her through the rusty little grating, which was Lord Bateman's only source of light and air. The prisoner was singing a melancholy song to keep himself company; and these were the words of it:

> *My hounds they all run masterless,*
> *My hawks they fly from tree to tree,*
> *My youngest brother will have my lands,*
> *Fair England again I'll never see!*

The sad words, and the sad tune of it, filled Susie Pye's heart with pity for the young prisoner, and she called gently to him, 'Is it true, sir, that the whole of Northumberland belongs to you? How much of it would you give to a fair young lady who would free you from your prison?'

Through the grating, Lord Bateman replied, 'Half Northumberland belongs to me, but I have further lands, and houses, a Hall near London, and other castles as well. I would gladly give all to the fair young lady who sets me free!'

So then Susie bent down low and whispered, 'I will make a

vow, that if in seven years you wed no other woman, then I in seven years, will wed no other man.'

Next she ran barefoot to her father's bedroom, where she stole the keys that lay beneath the silken pillow; then she tip-toed to the cellar and the pantry to fetch wine and spice-cake.

Silently she ran back to the dungeon where there were three heavy doors to unlock, and stern warders to bribe with gold before she came to the inner cell where Lord Bateman lay.

The young lord looked a sorry sight, for he was lean with seven years' hunger, was unshaved, and the rats and mice had nibbled his golden hair while he slept. But even all that could not conceal his handsome features, or the love and gratitude in the look he gave Susie Pye.

She gave him the cake. She gave him the wine. She sent for a comb for his hair, and a razor for his beard. She put five hundred pounds in his pocket. And, best of all, she took the gold ring from her finger, broke it in two, and gave one half to him. And she prayed that he would return to her when seven years were gone.

Then, when dusk fell, she led him down to the harbour. There she set him in one of her father's fine ships, and paid the sailors handsomely, and waved him away to Northumberland.

Now when seven years and fourteen days were gone, faithful Susie Pye packed up her finest clothes and went down to the harbour again. This time it was herself setting sail for England.

When the voyage was ended, and the ship approached the Northumbrian shore, a faint pealing of bells was blown across the North Sea. The Turkish crew saw a beautiful country spreading out before them, with splendid castles, and broad fields where herds of cattle and flocks of sheep grazed peacefully.

As soon as the ship landed, Susie Pye ran across the shore and up a narrow path to the low cliff-top; and as she went the bells rang louder, and more joyfully.

She saw a shepherd driving his flock, and asked him whose it was and whose were the fat cattle, and who lived in the turreted castle on the hill?

The shepherd replied, 'They are all Lord Bateman's flocks and herds, and all the land you see, and far beyond, is his; for he owns half Northumberland. The bells you hear ringing are wedding bells, for today Lord Bateman is to be married in his castle on the hill.'

Susie Pye was breathless when she reached the castle gate, and rattled at the latch. Then, when the porter came to open up, she gave him three golden guineas for himself, and, taking her half-ring from her pocket, she begged him to deliver it to his master.

The astonished porter took it from her, and went to the hall where Lord Bateman was with his bride, and all the bridal guests. And he told his lord of the young girl who stood at the gate—and he swore that in all the thirty-three years he had kept the castle-gate, never had he seen such a beautiful lady as this one was.

Now the mother of the bride was standing by, and she rebuked the porter for saying such a thing, for she believed, as so many mothers do, that no one could be more beautiful than her own daughter.

But the porter would not be denied, and insisted that the fair young girl had no equal.

'And,' he added, 'her fine clothing alone, would buy all Northumberland, and her golden girdle would be worth the price of an earldom. She wears a ring on every finger, and on her middle finger she wears three. But this half-ring she sends to you, my lord,' and he handed the half of Susie Pye's ring to Lord Bateman.

No sooner had Lord Bateman recognised the ring than he bounded down the staircase, five steps at a time, so anxious was he to see Susie Pye and hold her in his arms.

At first proud Susie turned her head away, so that he could not see her tears. 'Now farewell, Lord Bateman!' she cried. 'I will try to think of you no more.'

But he would not let her go, and swore that she had not come too late, for he would marry none but her who had come so far, and done so much for him.

So Lord Bateman's wedding that had started with one bride, finished with another. It was natural enough that the first bride, and her proud mother, should be disgruntled at the turn that had been taken. But Lord Bateman did what he could to make amends. His rejected bride had come to him riding humbly on horseback—so he sent her home in a handsome coach and three. She had brought her dowry in a linen purse—and he sent her home with double-dowry in a silk one.

Then he took his own bonny love by the hand, and changed her name from Susie Pye to Lady Joan, and the bells rang out joyfully again across the whole of Northumberland.

CALLALY CASTLE

A long time since, there was a lord and a lady who lived in a crumbling Northumbrian fortress called Callaly Castle.

They both agreed that what they needed was a fine new castle, but there the agreement ended. The lady wanted it to be built in the snug shelter of the valley, and the lord wanted it high on the top of the hill, and neither would give way to the other—not one inch!

So, for a long time it wasn't built anywhere at all, and the lord and his lady almost stopped speaking to one another except in barks and grunts.

At last the lord realised that if he waited for his wife to change her mind, he would be waiting from now till Kingdom Come. So he decided to set the builders to work on his chosen hill-top, and if his lady didn't like it she could stay where she was and learn to be happy with what she had.

Without another word to his wife on the subject plans were drawn, measurements were made, stone was quarried nearby and piled on to the ox-carts, and the patient beasts struggled up the hill with it, where the foundations had been dug. For days the air was loud with the chink of metal on stone.

The Lord of Callaly strutted about, sometimes whistling, sometimes humming, admiring the view and getting in the way of the builders.

But the Lady of Callaly just kept busy with what she was doing, smiled to herself, and said nothing at all.

Slowly the walls began to rise, knee high, waist high, shoulder high.

The Lord of Callaly was delighted. He strutted about, humming more loudly, whistling more shrilly, finding the view even more splendid, and, no doubt, getting more in the way of the builders every day.

But the Lady of Callaly just kept busy with what she was doing, smiled to herself, and said nothing at all.

Then came a morning when the lord climbed up the hill and found to his astonishment and rage, that every stone that had been built up the day before, was now lying tumbled to the ground.

Calling the builders together, he berated them for their poor workmanship.

'My old castle stood for centuries,' he blustered, 'even though it is crumbling now. Am I to change it for a castle that cannot stand for half a day and one night? Did you learn nothing during your apprenticeships? A child playing with toy bricks could have done better! Nincompoops! Jobbernowls! Ne'er-do-weels! Worms! Dullards! Witlings! Mumps!' And he swore seven old-fashioned oaths, one after the other—and then began again.

The builders, huddled together, shook with fear of some terrible punishment, and apologised, and blamed the masons who had dressed the stones. The masons in turn, blamed the quarrymen, and all promised to work more carefully in the future.

Everyone that day, worked fast and feverishly to repair the ruin of the day before.

But their efforts were utterly wasted. Next night the same thing happened, and the night after that—and that. As fast as the walls were built up by day, so fast were they tumbled down by night.

Although he went on blaming and shouting and blustering, the Lord of Callaly's own eyes could find no fault in his builder's work. Someone, or something, was making wrack and ruin of all their skill. He made up his mind to find the cause of the nightly downfall.

So he ordered the master builder to hide in an old shepherd's hut, with a boy for company, to watch the haunted site from dusk to dawn.

The two of them settled down to wait, with a flagon of ale for warmth, and a pair of pitchforks for protection against any marauders.

At midnight, when the moon was high, a hollow voice was heard chanting,

Callaly Castle stands on a height
Up by day, and down by night,
Set it down by the Shepherd's haugh
There it shall stand and never fa'!

And above the horizon there bristled a devilish creature, terrible beyond belief, taller than a man, blacker than night, with gleaming white tusks.

Shivery-shaky-prickly-knee'd, the master builder and his boy saw the thing rise on its hind legs and begin to pull down the building stone by stone, with what would have been hands if they had belonged to a man instead of a fiend.

Maybe the moonlight and the shadows and the ale added to the terror of the watchers and exaggerated the size of the monster—and maybe it was only a tall trusted servant of the Lady of Callaly carrying out her orders, dressed in the skin of a wild boar—for an enormous boar had been killed in the forest in the spring of that year. But certain it was that those two watchers felt sure that it was Owd Scrat himself who was hurling the stones after them, as, dropping their pitchforks, they fled down the slope of Callaly Hill. And certain it is, that no builder could be persuaded to work on that hilltop ever again.

So there in the low land of Shepherd's Haugh stands Callaly Castle today. And all the lord could do was to pretend that that was where he had always intended it to be, and that the notion of a castle on the hilltop was not a passing fancy, but a sensible demonstration to his household, of how unsuitable such a site would be.

But the Lady of Callaly just kept busy with what she was doing, smiled to herself, and said nothing at all.

THE LAIDLEY WORM OF SPINDLESTONE HEUGH

Long ago in the days of the Seven Kingdoms, before there were any counties, the royal castle of Bamburgh, founded on a great basalt rock, was perched right on the edge of a Kingdom. On one side the North Sea ebbed and flowed. On the other side lay the whole of Northumbria. At one time it might have been called Joyous Garde, for it was believed to be the castle given by King Arthur to Sir Lancelot.

Below the rock, when the tide was out, there were sea anemones in pools, and star fish, and little crabs left on the pale fine sand.

There the royal children could play, and dig for treasure, and look out across the water towards Denmark, and try to count the treacherous Farne Islands where the demons used to live before Saint Cuthbert drove them all away. But there were always fewer, or more islands than they thought there were, as the tides took turns to hide or seek the smallest ones. The islands had ferocious-sounding names like Fang, and Crumstone, and the Wamses, and Glororum Shad—and one had no name at all, and is still called the Nameless Rock because no one has ever thought of a name for it.

When the tide was in, the sea anemones, and the star fish and the little crabs were deeply covered by the water. Then, on some gentle days, the North Sea slapped and stroked and chattered at the bottom of the castle rock. But mostly it boomed and roared and pounded, bouncing its salty spray up towards the battlements of the castle.

Growing on the rock, all around the castle, there were hummocks of pink sea-thrift, and sea-campion, and tiny land snails with stripy shells. High above there was fresh air and blue sky, with fat rounded clouds blowing across; and there were always herring-gulls, and sometimes swallows, swooping and gliding.

But there was once a King of Northumbria who was sad and lonely, although he lived in such a beautiful place.

He had a brave and handsome son called Childe Wynd. 'Childe' in those days, was a title given to a young nobleman before he became a knight. Childe Wynd had sailed away across the sea as soon as he was old enough, in search of adventure.

And the King had a daughter, Margaret. She was kind and lovely through and through, as her mother had been before her. She kept her father company and ordered all the work of the castle, tripping out, and tripping in, with the keys hanging over her left shoulder. She was so considerate and polite to the servants that they never asked for a rise in wages, or wanted to work for anyone else.

But her good character, and her good looks, were always a sad reminder to the King of his Queen who had died many years before.

The King had always declared that he would never, never marry again, because he could never love anyone as he had loved his first Queen.

But one day when he was away on his travels, he met a dark-eyed beauty, fell head over ears in love with her, and asked her, there and then, to be his bride.

And she said, 'Thank you,' and 'I will.'

Great was the surprise at Bamburgh when news reached the Princess and the household, that the King was bringing home a new Queen.

What a polishing and scrubbing there was then! What a strewing of fresh rushes! What bed-making! What a shaking-up of pillows! And what baking! What roasting and boiling and toasting! What appetising smells floated from the kitchen to greet the King and his new Queen!

Margaret, who had long been the sole mistress of the castle, might have been forgiven if she had felt a little unwilling to hand over all her privileges to a total stranger. But she had a generous nature, and gave no sign of envy or disappointment when she went with her ladies to welcome her father and stepmother at the castle gate.

Behind the Princess, the servants crowded on tip-toe, peering and craning their necks to catch a glimpse of their new mistress. She was, indeed, someone to be gaped at! Tall and extraordinarily handsome, with her fine white skin and jet black hair, she walked proudly in her stiff silken gown that rustle-me-tustled as she moved.

The Princess, making a deep curtsey, handed over the castle keys to their new owner, saying quietly,

'O welcome, father dear, to your halls and bowers;

And welcome to you my new mother

For all that's here is yours.'

No sooner had she spoken, than one of the King's knights exclaimed, far too loudly, 'We have a handsome queen now, without doubt, but even she is not so beautiful as our own princess!'

Now, what he said might well have been true; but it was not a good thing to say while standing so close to the Queen who had extremely sharp ears for what she was not intended to hear.

'So that is what they think!' she said to herself. She would put an end to Margaret's beauty, she would! She stamped and shouted and worked herself up into a rare old tantrum, cursing and swearing as only a wicked witch could curse—for that is what she was—as wicked a witch as a witch could be!

It might seem unlikely for a witch to be as handsome as that queen appeared to be. But that was all part of the wicked magic with which she had bewitched the King of Northumbria into marrying her. Her beauty was only skin deep; inside she was spiky, and dangerous and evil. She lost no time in casting one of her spiteful spells, for on that very night, the Princess disappeared.

High and low they looked for her, calling her name, and peering with lanterns into every cranny of the castle. In the morning they scanned the sea and searched the shore, dreading that she had fallen from the castle rock and drowned in the waves below. Week after week they went on looking, until all hope was gone.

Only the jealous Queen, smiling serenely to herself, knew what had happened to Margaret, and she, you may be sure, wasn't telling.

Three miles away from Bamburgh Castle, at Spindlestone Heugh, there was an inland cave. And just at that time a laidley worm suddenly appeared in the cave—come from nowhere, but seeming to be there to stay. A 'laidley worm' means a loathsome worm, a nasty, repulsive, abominable sort of worm, and a 'worm' in those days, and in that place, was the name for a serpent.

Every day the serpenty worm grew bigger and bigger, and more and more laidley.

In the daytime, it slept snoring in the cave, but at night it came wriggling out, and devoured the crops of the fields and gardens of the neighbourhood. What it did not eat was shrivelled by the poison it spat or dribbled from its gummy chops. For seven miles east, and seven miles west, and seven miles north and south, not a blade of grass nor corn could be seen.

There were no more hummocks of pink thrift to be found growing on the rock, and when the laidley worm crawled and slithered along the shore, the little crabs scuttered back into the sea.

There was a great stone trough outside the Spindlestone cave, and every day frightened villagers filled the trough with the milk from seven stately cows, to fill the greedy stomach of the worm. This took away something of its hunger, but famine still threatened that part of the Kingdom, and people still mourned the loss of their princess.

At last, news of their plight reached the young prince, Childe Wynd. He swore a great oath that he would return home and slay the laidley worm, and avenge his sister Margaret; for he had the second sight and knew, even from a great distance, that the Queen's witchcraft had caused the disappearance of the princess.

Childe Wynd gathered together thirty-three faithful friends, and they built a long strong ship with masts of rowan wood, for rowan wood is a sure defence against every kind of evil and witchcraft; and there were fine silken sails, as red as rowan berries. For seven days and seven nights they sailed, till they came in sight of the Kingdom.

Just as Childe Wynd sighted his homeland, the Queen, who was sewing in her room, looked from the window and saw the strange red-sailed ship, sailing serenely through the treacherous Farne Islands.

She was angry and frightened, because she felt in her witchy bones that this was a ship of ill-omen for her, and that Childe Wynd would be her downfall.

So she called together her coven of witch-wives, cantankerous old hags with insides as evil as her own, and outsides worse than gargoyles.

'Fly to that ship,' she ordered them. 'Bore a hole in the hull, or raise fierce storms so that Childe Wynd will never reach the land.'

Away flew the witch-wives on the back of the wind, but as they approached the ship they felt their power dwindling away through their toes and finger-ends, for none of their spells could work against a ship with masts of rowan. So they turned themselves round about, and waited feebly for the wind to change, and drift them back sulking to the Queen.

She, furious at their failure, sent out a boat-load of men-at-arms to attack the dreaded ship. But they met with even less success than the witch-wives, for their boat returned only a few minutes after they set out.

Then the Queen saw that Childe Wynd was fast approaching the harbour. Quickly she drew the laidley worm to the water's edge by her magic power; and from there it floundered into the sea, lashing its tail and heaving the water into great mountains and valleys, so that the ship was tossed like a leaf from side to side.

Three times Childe Wynd and his three and thirty brave sailors tried to row ashore, and three times they were thrust back by the furious sea, stirred by the laidley worm.

At last the Queen, watching from her bower window, saw the ship retreating towards the horizon. Thinking she had seen the last of Childe Wynd, she turned away from the sight of the sea, and smiling contentedly she picked up her embroidery again.

But that was not the last of Childe Wynd. He turned his ship about, and rounded the next point, bringing her into the shallow waters of Budle Bay, where the wading birds paddle at the water's edge.

There he landed, mounted his horse, and speedily sought out the laidley worm. He drew his sword and was about to cut off its head when, to his amazement it spoke to him with human speech, and said,

'O quit your sword, unbend your bow,
And give me kisses three.
For though I am a poisonous worm
No harm I'll do to thee.'

Childe Wynd was astonished, not only that the worm should speak at all, but that it spoke with the voice of his lost sister Margaret.

Then the worm spoke again,

'O quit your sword, unbend your bow,
And give me kisses three.
If I'm not won ere set of sun
Won never shall I be.'

Anyone else might have hesitated to do such a thing, but the knight immediately kissed the worm fairly and squarely on its brow.

Nothing happened.

He kissed it a second time.

It still seemed to be a laidley worm.

Then he kissed it a third time, and it hissed, and roared, and disappeared, leaving in its place, the King's lovely daughter Margaret!

The Prince wrapped his cloak around her, set her on his horse, and together they nick-a-ti-nacked at full speed to Bamburgh Castle.

There, you may be sure, was more kissing, and some hugging as well. The old king was beside himself with joy, and once more there were appetising smells wafting out of the kitchen as a great banquet of celebration was prepared.

There were even greater celebrations later, when Margaret was married to the outspoken knight who had been so charmed by her beauty on the day when the Queen first came to Bamburgh.

As for that troublesome queen, what she had done to the princess, was now done to her.

Childe Wynd touched her with a twig of rowan tree, and as he did so, she shrank and shrank, and her skin loosened till she became a squatting, crawling, hissing, spitting, waddling toad—a laidley toad, with only the bright shining of her eyes left as a reminder of what she once had been.

She hid herself in the bottom of the well in the castle keep; the well that is still there today, though the laidley toad has not been seen for many a year.

The land recovered from the scorching breath of the laidley worm, and became fertile again. Hummocks of pink thrift, and sea-campion, and little land snails with stripy shells grew once more on the castle rock.

The sea anemones waved their tentacles happily in the pools, and there were star fish again, and little crabs on the sand. Peace and happiness came back to the Kingdom of Northumbria.

KING ARTHUR AND THE
SHEPHERD OF SEWINGSHIELDS

Most people agree that when King Arthur died, he drifted away in a barge, across a great lake, and vanished into the sunrise. But there is much disagreement about what happened afterwards.

Some will tell you that he was buried in Glastonbury, away down in the west country, the place believed to be Avalon. A Welshman would likely tell you that the King was brought to life again by his half-sister Morgan le Fay, and then spirited away to Wales where he sleeps in a cave beneath a hazel tree on Craig-y-Dinas until his country has need of him. While the Scots have it that the cavern lies beneath their Eildon Hills. And a Yorkshire-man will insist that it is under Richmond Castle that King Arthur is sleeping.

But you ask a Northumbrian, and he will tell you that all these others are mistaken. He will tell you that King Arthur and his Queen, and the Knights of the Round Table, and their Ladies and their hounds as well, are certainly still asleep, in a great underground chamber at Sewingshields, up there by the Roman Wall. And to prove what he says is true, he will tell you this story.

There was once, years ago, a shepherd; and like all the Northumbrian shepherds before him, and many since, he was a great knitter. For who has greater need of good warm stockings than a shepherd out on the cold hills? And what can keep your fingers better occupied than knitting yourself a pair, while your head and legs are busy minding those hardy little dark-faced sheep who so kindly provide the wool for them?

One day the shepherd had gone up to Sewingshields. The old castle that used to be there, had long since fallen into ruin. Finding his flock where they ought to be, and doing what they should, and with time enough to get home before dark, he sat down among the ruins for a few minutes to turn the heel of his stocking, for that was the only part of his knitting that needed his full attention. He could do the rest of it blindfold, standing on his head. He had not done a dozen stitches before the ball of wool slipped from his lap and rolled away into some brambles.

The shepherd said a bad word or two, put the knitting into his pocket, and got up to seek his ball which had quite disappeared down a gully between nettles and brambles. Following his strand of wool, he was led downward into a gloomy underground passage.

'A-ha!' he thought to himself. 'Could this be the entrance to that underground hall where King Arthur sleeps with all his Knights?' For his grandmother had told him the story of King Arthur and his Round Table, and the enchanted sleepers beneath the Roman Wall.

At first he pressed on eagerly through the dim green light of the narrow passage. But it was cold, and a slimy wetness trickled down the rocky walls. Squatty toads with down-turned mouths, and lizards, shuffled across the floor in front of him. Stinkhorns, and other fungi gave out a stench of rottenness and decay. Bats, hanging from the low ceiling, tangled in his hair, and some damp indefinite creature slithered down his back. An overgrown rat, scuttling across the passage, ran over his foot.

The shepherd might have turned back, if it had not been for the brightness glowing far ahead of him. Groping towards it, he stumbled on through that hideous corridor, until he found himself in a great hall ablaze with light.

The brightness came not only from a magnificent silver lamp hanging from the ceiling, but from a mysterious flame, which seemed to spring from the floor. No fuel fed this pure white flame nor was the floor beneath it charred by its heat.

All around the hall, on costly chairs and couches, were knights in armour, with their ladies in robes of a time gone by. In the centre of them, on a high throne was a crowned King, his Queen by his side. At their feet lay thirty couple of hounds. Every man and woman and beast was in a profound sleep, and the shepherd could hear nothing but his own breathing, and the thumping of his heart.

There on a carved table in front of the King lay the means to waken them from that enchanted sleep—King Arthur's sword Excalibur, a silken garter, and a bugle horn.

'Just as my grandmother told me,' whispered the shepherd. 'The sword, the garter, and the horn. To draw the sword—that is the first thing!'

Cautiously he approached the table, and lifted the great jewelled sword in its heavy scabbard. Slowly he drew out the sword, and as he did so there was a breathing, and a rustling, and a silken whispering as the knights and ladies lazily opened their eyes and began to sit themselves upright. There was a fidgeting and a grinding of teeth among the hounds. The shepherd felt poor and shabby among so much splendour.

'To cut the garter—that is the second thing!' he said to himself as he slashed the garter in two with the sharp sword.

But that done, he began to have misgivings. These noblemen who had lain here for centuries, neither dead nor properly alive, what would they do when they woke to find an intruder in their court? What would he answer if they asked him why their enchanted sleep had been disturbed? How was he to know if the time was ripe for King Arthur to return to the living world? What could one unarmed shepherd do before so many knights in armour if they took against him? And what if those grumbling hounds bared their teeth? A dozen other fears and doubts began chasing round inside the shepherd's head.

Quickly he slipped the great sword back into the scabbard. He would get out of this grisly place. It was making his flesh creep. He would come back another day, now that he had found the way in. He would come back better prepared, with friends to help him, in case of any danger.

No sooner was the sword sinking back into its sheath, than that strange company began to sink back on their chairs and couches, and droop once more into their deathlike sleep.

But the shepherd did not wait. Before the stillness was complete he had turned and fled along the reptile-haunted passage that would take him back to daylight, and hills, and sky. As he fled he heard the deep drowsy voice of King Arthur calling after him:

'Oh woe betide the evil day
On which the witless wight was born,
Who drew the sword, the garter cut,
But never blew the bugle horn!'

After that there was a silence—a silence that has not yet been broken. When the shepherd reached the ground above, he was berated by family and friends alike for having lost heart so readily, and fearing, or forgetting, to blow the bugle horn.

'You fool!' said his brothers. 'You silly fool!'

'You coward!' said the neighbours. 'You dithering coward!'

And there was a score who would go back with him there and then, along that dreadful passage, to do what was needed to break the charm. But neither he, nor they, were able to find the secret entrance ever again, though they searched all that day, and many a day after.

So there they all are, King Arthur, Queen Guinevere, the Knights and their Ladies, and thirty couple of hounds, waiting still, somewhere beneath Sewingshields, for someone to draw the sword, cut the garter, and blow the bugle horn.

The Hedley Kow

There was at one time, an ill-willy bogy-beast living in the neighbourhood of Hedley, in County Durham. It was called the Hedley Kow.

The villagers of Hedley spelt it with a 'K' to avoid confusion with any of their homely Durham cushie-cows which were always spelt with a 'c'—for confusion was one of the Kow's favourite mischiefs. It was continually changing itself into a horse, or a cow (especially a cow) or a donkey, or somebody's sweetheart, or a bundle of sticks, or anything else it fancied—for no good reason except its own amusement, and the bewilderment and annoyance of the neighbours. It was never the same shape for two days together. That is why there are so many different stories about the Hedley Kow.

Sometimes it would lie down on a lonely stretch of road, and turn itself into a truss of straw. Then some old wife would surely come along, and, seeing the straw lying there, would toss it up on her shoulders thinking,

'Findie, findie, keeps it,
Losie, losie, seeks it!'

and set off towards home, well pleased with her find.

Before she had gone many steps, the straw would become heavier and heavier, and heavier, until the poor old soul would have to lay it down to rest her aching back and shoulders, and to gasp for breath.

No sooner was the straw on the ground again than it would jump itself upright, and shuffle down the lane in front of the old woman, swinging first to one side, and then to the other. Every now and again it would give a shout or guffaw, just like a living thing, which was not surprising considering it was really the Hedley Kow, but very surprising and alarming for the old body who thought there was nothing in the road but herself and a lifeless bundle of straw!

At last there would be a sound like the rushing of a whirlwind, and the straw that was the Kow (or the Kow that was the straw) would vanish altogether—until the next time!

Now there was a farmer living at the High Field called Jemmy Brown. Jemmy had spent all his working life in that place, and knew all the countryside round about like the back of his own hand.

He always boasted that he was by no means a nervous sort of man; but for all that, he always quickened his pace on that lonely stretch of road where the Hedley Kow was known to play so many of its tricks—the very same stretch of road where the Kow

had teased more than one old woman with a truss of straw.

Jemmy was trotting home one bogleish night, when the wind was wailing and blowing the clouds so quickly across the moon's face that the shadows seemed forever jumping out sideways at him. The long skinny fingers of the creaking ash trees rattled above. Dry leaves somersaulted along the road ahead, and in the wood on either side of the road, invisible things snapped, and coughed, and tu-whooed. The clop-clopping of his horse's hooves echoed behind him.

Jemmy was recollecting the most recent stories he had heard about the Hedley Kow. Last week he and his neighbour, Matt Robson, had been laughing heartily about them. The Kow's pranks, played on gullible, ignorant victims, seemed funny enough then in good company in the warm alehouse. They didn't seem so funny now that he was in that echoing storm by himself, in the narrow lane that was known to be the favourite playground of the Hedley Kow.

He wished that he had some friendly human company now that the storm clouds were lowering, and the moon was quite blotted out.

After rounding a bend in the road, Jemmy was comforted to see, through the blackness, a figure ahead of him, also jogging along on horseback.

It was too dark for recognising detail, but Jemmy didn't care whether it was friend or stranger. It would be good to have a travelling companion for the rest of the road. So he urged on his horse to catch up with the rider in front.

Now the rider in front had also boasted that he was by no means a nervous sort of man, but, for all that, he always quickened his pace on that lonely stretch of road where the Kow was known to play so many of its tricks.

He, too, heard the skinny fingers of the creaking ash trees rattling above, and the rustling of the dry leaves as they somersaulted on the road ahead; and the snapping and coughing and tu-whooing of the invisible things in the wood on either side of the road, and the echo of the clop-clopping of his own horse's hooves behind him.

But he thought he could hear something else as well. He thought he could hear the clop-clopping of some other horse behind him. And he fell to thinking about thieves on horseback, and highwaymen, and fly-by-nights. So he urged on his own horse.

Jemmy Brown, finding that he was making no ground at all, spurred on *his* horse, in turn.

The rider in front, fearing that the thief on horseback, or highwayman, or fly-by-night was gaining on him, spurred on his poor horse, harder.

Jemmy Brown, now in a frenzy at finding himself losing, instead of gaining ground, shouted

'Stop! Stop! Stop!' as he upped with his bottom, and downed with his head, whipping and spurring his poor horse in the effort to catch up with the galloping horseman in front.

The galloping horseman in front, hearing the shouts and the thundering hooves behind him, was sure that no common thief would be advertising his whereabouts so loudly. Convinced that only the Hedley Kow or some other malevolent spirit could be pursuing him, he upped with *his* bottom, and downed with *his* head, whipping and spurring his horse to still greater effort.

So it was that Jemmy Brown and the rider in front spurred and whipped for close on two more miles, the sweat running out of man and beast till there was no more sweat left to run.

At last, the rider in front, finding that his pursuer was now gaining on him, decided that it must indeed be an evil spirit that was following behind; something far more sinister than the Hedley Kow, or a common brownie playing a prank. Maybe it was Beelzebub himself, and only the power of heaven could save him from such evil clutches.

Abruptly, he pulled up his horse, and facing the supposed evil spirit, he called out, 'In the name of the Father, and of the Son, and of the Holy Ghost, who art thou?'

Instead of an evil spirit, a horrified neighbour answered, repeating the question, 'I is Jemmy Brown o' the High Field. Who's thou?'

But Jemmy Brown didn't need an answer to his question, for the wind, at that moment, blew the cloud away from the moon, and its light shone on the homely but terrified features of his good friend and neighbour Matt Robson.

Something invisible was yaffling in the wood, at the side of the road, holding its invisible sides with laughter; and it wouldn't surprise me at all if it was the Hedley Kow.

THE CAULD LAD OF HYLTON

There are some people who think that the Cauld Lad of Hylton was a brownie. That would be likely enough, for there were brownies all over the north-east of England at one time. But some swore he was a goblin, and others believed he was the ghost of a poor little stable lad who was murdered with a hayfork by one of the Lords of Hylton and then tossed into a pond.

But whatever else he may have been, or may not have been, this much is certain—he was no more than three feet high, with a dark skin and a shaggy head, and if he wore any clothes at all, they were poor thin useless rags, or why else would he be a cauld lad?

Now sometimes the Cauld Lad would come into the kitchen of Hylton Castle late at night when all the servants had gone up to their beds. Then he would warm himself by sweeping the floor, scouring the pots and kettles, sharpening the knives, straightening all that was crooked, leaving the place as tidy as tidy could be, ready for morning. That is the way brownies usually do behave.

Other times he would warm himself by smashing the plates and dishes, tipping salt into the flour, shaking so much pepper into the soup that the children nearly sneezed the noses off their astonished little faces, pouring water all over the fire logs, and leaving the place all hugger-mugger for the morning. And that is the way goblins usually do behave.

For the Cauld Lad was a contrary lad, and whichever way the kitchen was left, he would have it otherwise. So it was hardly surprising that the kitchen maids often left it untidy on purpose, so that the Cauld Lad could clean it before morning, if he felt so inclined. And who is there wouldn't do the same in their place?

Yet on other nights, he neither tidied nor untidied, but kept the housekeeper awake by singing in a thin, melancholy voice,

> *Wae's me, wae's me,*
> *The acorn's not yet*
> *Fallen from the tree*
> *That's to grow the wood*
> *That's to make the cradle,*
> *That's to rock the bairn,*
> *That's to grow to a man,*
> *That's to lay me.*

which is more like the way a small shivering ghost behaves, than a brownie or a goblin.

At last a time came when the housekeeper thought it was a shame that the maids were being paid for work they didn't do, and she was rather sorry for the Cauld Lad, but at the same time tired of being kept awake by his mournful singing. So she went to the hen-wife who knew more than most about such things, and asked, 'Can you tell me any way of getting rid of that Cauld Lad?'

And the hen-wife said, 'Easy! Easy as easy can be! All you have to do is to give him some clothes to cover his bareness, and you'll no longer be troubled by him.'

So the housekeeper found a piece of green cloth, and she cut and snipped and stitched it into a splendid little cloak with a hood to match. And she made a little suit and a shirt with some left-overs that she had.

When everything was ready, and the lazy maids had left all the cleaning-up and gone to bed, she laid the little clothes in front of the fire to warm, and hid herself in the broom cupboard with a small scullery maid for company. It was very dark in the cupboard, but they left the door open, just a chink, so that they could watch the goings-on in the firelight.

Then, on the stroke of midnight, although they hadn't taken their eyes off the hearth, there was the Cauld Lad standing in front of the fire; and neither of them had seen him come in, yet both were certain that he hadn't been there the minute before.

Even from the back, the little fellow looked very happy staring at the brownie-sized garments.

Very, very slowly he put them on; the shirt, the breeches, the waistcoat and the jacket; then, last of all, the splendid green cloak with the hood to match. They all fitted perfectly.

The Cauld Lad was delighted with himself. All over the kitchen he frisked, taking no notice of the dirty pans that were standing on the floor, except to leap over them, and scattering dirty linen from the basket, like overgrown snowflakes all round the room; lively as a flea, cutting summersets and gambadoes, which is an old-fashioned, but very satisfactory way of being joyful.

It was quite clear to the watchers in the cupboard that the Cauld Lad had no intention of doing any work *that* night.

Nor did he, for at the first cock-crow, calling out,

'Here's a cloak, and here's a hood,

The Cauld Lad of Hylton will do *no more good*!'
he took a final leap into nowhere, and was never seen again.

So the kitchen maids of Hylton Castle had to do all the dirty work themselves next morning, and for ever afterwards.

THE JI-JALLER BAG

There was once an old woman who lived by herself, in a cottage that was not far from Newcastle-upon-Tyne.

Maybe this old woman was a witch—and maybe she wasn't; or, perhaps she was a miser or a thief, because she had something hidden in her cottage that she didn't want anyone to know about. You must make up your own mind about it.

As she grew older her rheumatism worsened, and she began to find it hard to get through all her housework, so she hired a pretty little servant girl to help her with it.

Then, while the clock ticked, and the cat purred on the hearth-rug, the old woman put her feet up and took things easily for a time.

But on the very first evening, she said to the girl, 'Tomorrow you must rise early, and sweep out every corner of the house, but be sure *never* to put your sweeping brush up the chimney.'

Next day the girl rose early, as she had been told, and swept the house clean in every corner; but, of course, she didn't put the sweeping brush up the chimney, which was the last thing she would have thought of doing.

Then in the evening, the old woman said to her, just as she had said the day before, 'Tomorrow you must rise early and sweep out every corner of the house, but be sure *never* to put your sweeping brush up the chimney.'

And so it was, that every single evening the old woman told the girl exactly the same thing.

And every morning the girl did just what she had been told to do the day before; and she didn't do what she had been told not to do.

But, of course, the day came, as it was bound to come, when the girl wanted, more than anything in the world, to put that sweeping brush up that chimney. It was only human nature.

And, of course, soon after that, came the day when the little servant girl *did* put her sweeping brush up that chimney. And down fell a shower of soot and a long leather bag full of money.

The girl picked up the long leather bag, and popped it inside a ji-jaller bag that was hanging on a nail beside the chimney. If you know what a ji-jaller bag is like, you know more than I do. But that way, it kept the soot from rubbing off on her gown, and away she ran, out of the house, with the ji-jaller bag under her arm.

She had run some way when she came to a gate. The gate said to her, 'Pretty maiden will you open me, for I have not been opened for many a long year.'

But the girl tossed her curls, stuck her nose in the air, and said,

'Open yourself! . . . I have no time.'

She had run some way further, when she came to a gentle cow, chewing the meadow flowers. The cow said to her, 'Pretty maiden, stop and milk me, for I have not been milked for many a day.'

But the girl tossed her curls, stuck her nose in the air, and said,

'Milk yourself! . . . I have no time.'

She had run some way further when she came to a corn-mill. The mill said to her, 'Pretty maiden, will you turn me, for I haven't been turned for many a year.'

But the girl tossed her curls, stuck her nose in the air, and said,

'Turn yourself! . . . I have no time.'

The girl was very tired by this time, and her arms and legs were aching with so much carrying and so much running. So she hid the money bag and the ji-jaller bag inside the mill-hopper, and curled up on the hay in an empty barn, where she fell into a deep sleep.

When she woke up she had forgotten all about the old woman, and the money inside the long leather bag, inside the ji-jaller bag, inside the mill-hopper. So she ran off to her own mother, who was pleased enough to have the girl home again.

As soon as the old woman found the soot on the hearth, and her bag of money missing from the chimney, and the ji-jaller bag missing from its nail, she tottered off on her rheumaticky old legs to catch the little servant girl.

She went tottering on till she came to the gate, and she said, 'Gate o' mine, gate o' mine, have you seen a maid o' mine, with a ji-jaller bag, and a long leather bag with all the money in it that ever I had?'

But the gate just said, 'Farther on.'

So the old woman went tottering on till she came to the gentle cow, chewing the meadow flowers, and she said, 'Cow o' mine, cow o' mine, have you seen a maid o' mine, with a ji-jaller bag, and a long leather bag with all the money in it that ever I had?'

But the cow just said, 'Farther on.'

So the old woman went tottering on till she came to the corn-mill, and she said, 'Mill o' mine, mill o' mine, have you seen a maid o' mine, with a ji-jaller bag, and a long leather bag with all the money in it that ever I had?'

And the mill said, 'Look down the mill-hopper.'

So the old woman did look down the mill-hopper, and there sure enough, was the long leather bag of money inside the ji-jaller bag. So she stretched out her arm and grabbed them.

Once the money was safely in her grasp, the old woman didn't bother any more about chasing the servant girl, but hurried back home as fast as her stiff old legs would let her.

No sooner was she home than the long leather bag was poked up the chimney again, and the ji-jaller bag was hung back on its nail. The clock ticked, the cat purred on the hearth-rug, and the old woman put her feet up and took things easily for a time.

But it didn't last that way for long. With no one to help her, she again found it hard to get through her housework, so she set about finding another pretty little servant girl.

To this second one she said just what she had said to the first one, and she said it every day, 'Tomorrow you must rise early, and sweep out every corner of the house, but be sure *never* to put your sweeping brush up the chimney.'

Then, as before, the girl was obedient just until human nature got the better of her, and the day came, as it was bound to come, when she put the sweeping brush up the chimney and down fell the long leather bag of money!

And this girl, too, ran off with the long leather bag, and the ji-jaller bag, till she came to the gate.

And the gate said to her, just as it had said to the other girl, 'Pretty maiden, will you open me, for I have not been opened for many a long year.'

But this girl gave a very different answer from the first girl, for she smiled in a friendly way, and said, 'Certainly! Why not? It's no trouble at all!' And she opened the gate.

She gave the same answer to the gentle cow before she milked her, and to the mill before she turned it. Then she went on running till she came to where she wanted to be. And there she stopped.

Meanwhile the old woman, as you would expect, had set off after her. And when she came to the gate she said, 'Gate o' mine, gate o' mine, have you seen another maid o' mine, with a ji-jaller bag, and a long leather bag with all the money in it that ever I had?'

But the gate said absolutely nothing. And, what's more, the cow said absolutely nothing, and so did the mill. So, as far as I know, the old woman may still be running round Northumberland on her aching old legs, looking for the pretty little maid with the ji-jaller bag, and the long leather bag with all the money in it that ever she had.

Sir Walter the Bold

Once there was a young knight called Sir Walter—Sir Walter the Bold, who was famous throughout the Border for his bravery and skill at arms.

But one day, between the end of one Border skirmish and the beginning of the next, Sir Walter fell to thinking about his childhood, and remembering some of the old tales that his mother used to tell to him, and to his younger brothers. He particularly remembered a story of glittering treasure, hidden in a cave in the cliff beneath the old Priory of Tynemouth—and how the treasure was there to be claimed by any knight brave enough to fight the ghosts and dragons and other horrors who guarded it; and how many knights, thought to be brave, had entered that cave, but none, so far, had ever returned. And he remembered, to his shame, how, as a little boy, he had vowed to seek that treasure himself, just as soon as ever he was old enough to be a knight.

'And here I am,' Sir Walter said to himself, 'a knight twelve month and a day, and I have never thought about the Tynemouth treasure in all that time! My next brother will soon become a knight and maybe he will race me to that glorious but perilous adventure if I delay any longer.'

Now that day was the Eve of Saint John, and Saint John was the patron saint of Sir Walter the Bold. So he decided that if he was to be blessed on one day of the year more than another, the day of his patron saint would surely be the day.

So, wearing his heaviest armour, he set out without more ado and rode south and east, to Tynemouth.

It was already dark when he reached the coast, and a great summer storm was raging across the North Sea. Undaunted, Sir Walter began the slippery scramble up the rocks to the entrance of the cave, while the sea churned and roared and grumbled behind him. A flash of golden lightning showed him to be closer to the narrow entrance than he thought he was, and as a great roll of thunder echoed along the shore, with a single spring Sir Walter disappeared into that narrow sinister tunnel.

At first there were only the soft, slimy repulsive things that dropped and dribbled and oozed all round him. Sir Walter took no notice of them.

Then there were the yelling spirits that yelled louder and ever louder as the knight penetrated further into the labyrinth. The echo of their yelling mocked behind him, as blue flames flaring from their glassy eyeballs lit up the passage ahead.

'Quiet there!' shouted Sir Walter. 'If anyone disturbs the silence here, it shall be me!' He unsheathed his sword and sang a rollicking song to keep himself going as he slashed at the spectres to left and right; and the yelling, and the spectres, died away.

Then, in the darkness, he stumbled on some sluggish dragons that lay in his path.

'Out of my way!' he shouted. 'Where are your manners? I will teach you to block my way!' And he charged the surly lumps, hacking them down left and right with his sword, until the way was quite clear before him.

Next, there were the hell dogs. Sir Walter the Bold simply cut them in half as he came to them.

And in among the slimies and the yelling spirits, and the scaly dragons, and the hell dogs, there were stray bats, and bald crows, and hobgoblins, and rats, but they all howled and vanished at the brandishing of Sir Walter's sword.

A dim light was burning through the gloom ahead of him. Sir Walter made his way steadily towards it. Suddenly he paused. A great chasm yawned in front of him, so deep he could not see the bottom of it—and no bridge, nor anything he could use as a gangway to the other side.

Behind him, the ferocious creatures snickered with joy at his plight, but the young knight was not dismayed. Casting aside much of his heavy armour, but keeping his sword and helmet, he took a mighty leap and landed on the other side of the gulf. He wondered how many poor knights had missed their footing, and lay below in that treacherous gap.

But his trials were not over. For on the other side he was surrounded at once by hordes of indescribable monstrosities, such as he had never seen before, nor ever wished to see again.

He was sure now, that without the help of Heaven he could advance no further. So he knelt down and prayed that the good Saint John would come to his aid. Then he rose to his feet and pressed on towards the light with his head held high, though still pursued by a terrible noise, as though all the stones and rocks of Northumbria were falling around his ears.

At last he reached the burning light, and saw that his way was blocked by a huge wooden door. Above the door a bugle horn was hung by a golden chain. Walter the Bold took down the horn and blew three loud defiant blasts on it. As he did so the bugle turned into a hideous curling snake.

The bold Sir Walter instantly spat out the head before the snake could discharge the poison from its deadly fangs, and he stamped on it as it writhed on the ground. The sound of the horn roused a magic cockerel from the shadows, a beautiful gleaming bird, that crowed three times. And as it crowed all the indescribables dissolved away into the walls of the cave, and the great door swung open, revealing the hall of treasure.

Sir Walter held his breath as he gazed into the magnificent chamber that was upheld by twelve pillars of crystal, and twelve pillars of jasper; and at the twelve altars where incense was burning; and at all the diamonds and rubies and emeralds and sapphires that lay around in great chests, and spilled over on to the floor.

How much treasure Sir Walter took home with him, and how much he left behind him, has never been known to this day. Perhaps he made another journey to Tynemouth later, to get more of it.

But it is certain that he took out enough altogether to make him a very rich man indeed. For he bought a hundred castles and estates, so he could move to a different one twice a week, for almost a year, if that was the way his fancy took him. He built a monastery as well. He married a very beautiful and charming lady, and they lived together very happily for the rest of their lives.

The Black Dragon
of Longwitton

Near the tiny village of Longwitton, there were three wells of healing waters, known as Our Lady's Wells. Pilgrims travelled from far over the hills to drink at the wells and cure their sickness—especially those who had sore and watering eyes as the healing waters were particularly good for them.

In the days when brave knights jousted with other brave knights, or slew boars, or dragons, or laidley worms to prove their love for the bright-eyed ladies of their choice, a fearsome dragon came and settled himself close to those three holy wells.

The sight of the dragon was quite enough to stop villagers and strangers alike from visiting the wells. His skin was coal-black all over, rough and jagged, and underneath, from his belly-button to his chin, it was hard—so hard that no man could pierce it with sword or spear. His muscular neck was thick as a horse's neck, and his paws were like the paws of a lion but with claws that were even sharper and crueller. And how he could run! No horse in the King's tournament was swifter. If he didn't want to escape his enemies by running, then he would fly—for he had great scaly wings that could lift the huge weight of him skywards—and if he didn't want to escape by flying, he could make himself invisible and fool his enemies that way!

He was so strong and ferocious that he slew all he touched, both man and beast. It was no wonder that he had been neither killed nor captured, and that few folk dared to come within twenty miles of the wells of Longwitton and the dragon that guarded them.

Sometimes, when the dragon was in an invisible humour, he curled up in a deep sleep beside one of the wells. Then the villagers, seeing and hearing no sign of him, began to hope, and think that he had decided to leave Longwitton at last, and move away to worry someone else, somewhere else. Then, anxious to drink the healing waters once again, the bravest of them would make their way cautiously towards the wells.

But there was always someone who coughed, or sneezed, or trod on a loud-snapping stick, and the beast, angry at having his rest disturbed, would go rampaging round the wells, while the terrified villagers ran helter-skelter, tappy-lappy, back to their homes.

It was hard to say which was the more terrifying, to have the full sight of the dragon in all his turbulent fury, or to come un-awares on his invisibility—suddenly having the hot breath of him at the back of you, feeling the draught of him as he bellied through the undergrowth, seeing the bushes jostled by nobody, hearing the great wings flapping, and the squawking of terrified birds as the flying nothingness havocked through the rookery, shattering and scattering everything that was in the way of his flight through those upper reaches of the trees.

Many bold knights had determined to rid the country of the terrible scourge, and win their ladies' favour by slaying this troublesome dragon. One after another they fought bravely against it, and one after another, they were slain. Until at last, there was only one knight left in the whole of Northumberland. And he was barely old enough to be a knight, but he had made his vows and kept his vigil, and was as eager as all young men are, to prove that he was no longer a mere boy.

'Leave that dragon alone!' his mother said to him. 'There will be other nobler causes for you when you are a little older.'

But the fair and beautiful maiden whom he loved dearly, sighed, smiled, sighed again, and said to him, 'You are the last knight left in Northumberland! None of the others were brave enough, or strong enough, or clever enough to kill the dragon, so they were not worthy of my hand. How proud I should be to give my hand to the one who succeeds where all others failed!'

So, of course, that settled the matter for the young knight. He was, no doubt, very brave, and, no doubt, strong as any other healthy young man, but, perhaps, not quite as clever as he might be. For alas, although he battled courageously against the beast, he was tricked and confused by its sudden appearances and disappearances. The dragon felled the young man to the earth with a deadly blow from an invisible paw, and that, sadly, was the end of him.

So now there was not one knight left in the whole of Northumberland. And not all the water from Our Lady's Wells could have stopped the watering of his lovely lady's eyes when she heard the news.

There was no longer a king reigning in Northumbria. For, by that time, the seven kingdoms had been joined into one great kingdom, so that good King Athelstane ruled over the whole of England.

The Northumbrians sent word to King Athelstane, begging him to send an English knight from further south to kill their ferocious enemy.

The King considered all the bravest knights in his realm, and Sir Guy of Warwick seemed to be the most likely man.

For Sir Guy had dared many adventures at home, and in strange lands beyond the seas, to win the hand of his beautiful Phelis. He had already killed, single-handed, a lion, two giants, a wild boar, a dragon, and a monstrous and cruel beast called the Dun Cow of Dunsmore Heath. Furthermore, he had a wide knowledge of spells and enchantments.

So although that had been quite enough to win, and satisfy his lovely bride, he was still thirsty for further adventures, and was soon galloping northward at the King's request to challenge the Black Dragon of Longwitton.

When he came to Our Lady's Wells, there was the dragon sulking at the back of his den, his green eyes glinting through the gloom, and seeming in no mood to be disturbed.

Looking the beast straight in the eye, and using words and a voice that could not be disobeyed, Sir Guy called out, 'Come forth, wretched Dragon! Remain in your natural and visible shape, for you change it at your peril!' And the knight's power was so great that the dragon was no longer able to disappear. That was a good start. And if Sir Guy could prevent his disappearing, he could, no doubt, prevent his flying, by the same means.

But by this time, the dragon was pacing back and forth, displaying himself, as though accepting the challenge. It was now Sir Guy's task to kill him in fair fight.

That was harder to do than to tell, for the dragon seemed to have a charmed life. Bravely and skilfully Sir Guy slashed at him with his sharp sword, yet, though he sometimes drew blood, each wound closed immediately, and the dragon fought on, fresh as new. All the knight could do was to keep him at bay—until he noticed something. However much the dragon turned and twisted, the tip of his tail always trailed in the healing water of the holy well. So that was it! That was the source of the never-failing strength that closed his wounds!

Sir Guy would have to get that tail out of the water. With cunning and courage he drew the angry beast towards him by pretending to weaken and retreat. Then, when the pursuing dragon was almost on top of him, and a fair distance from the wells, like a stroke of greased lightning Sir Guy flashed down to the other end of him. Furiously, with his tail high in the air, the dragon turned to face his attacker, who now stood between him and the precious water.

But the dragon was powerless now, and when Sir Guy plunged his sword into him, nothing could stem the blood that flowed from the helpless creature.

So ended the Black Dragon of Longwitton, and Sir Guy of Warwick departed with another victory to add to his glorious adventures.

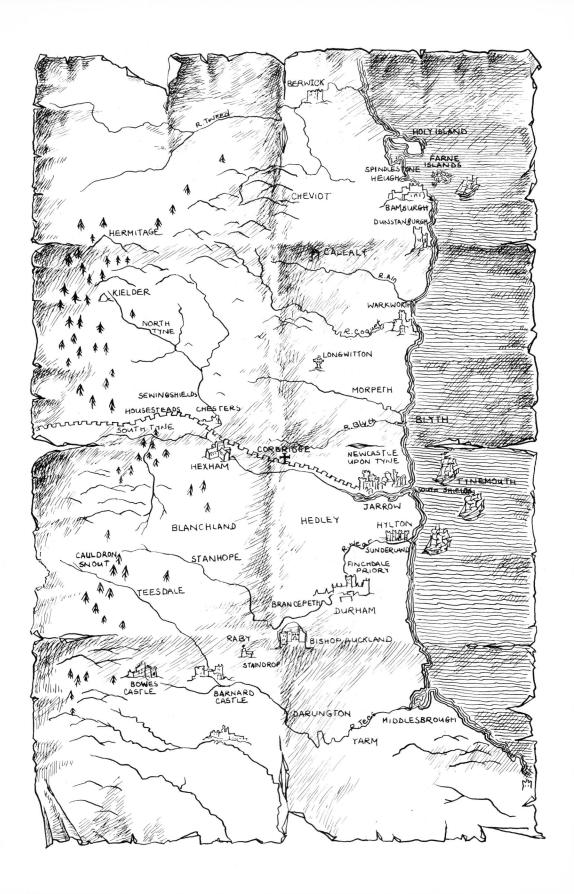